This Little Tiger book belongs to:

_____

_____

_____

For Raechele, who can never
have too much snow!
~ J C

LITTLE TIGER PRESS LTD,
an imprint of the Little Tiger Group
1 Coda Studios, 189 Munster Road, London SW6 6AW
Imported into the EEA by Penguin Random House Ireland,
Morrison Chambers, 32 Nassau Street, Dublin D02 YH68
www.littletiger.co.uk

First published in Great Britain 2019
This edition published 2019
Text and illustrations copyright © Jane Chapman 2019
Visit Jane Chapman at www.janekchapman.com

Printed in China • LTP/1400/4613/0422
4 6 8 10 9 7 5

The Snowiest Christmas Ever!

Jane Chapman

LITTLE TIGER

LONDON

It was very nearly Christmas.
The bears' cabin twinkled with decorations and,
all around the tree, parcels waited to be unwrapped.
Delicious smells wafted from the oven and the fire
crackled cosily.

All would be perfect were it not
for one thing . . .

"Snow!" squeaked Button, pointing at her storybook.
"PLEASE let there be snow this Christmas!
I want to see it for myself."

"Oh yes!" Mungo cried. "All fluffy and
soft for Santa's sleigh to land in!"

Papa laughed. "Don't worry, cubs,
I'm sure that snow is on the way."

But there was no snow
at bathtime.

And still no snow
at bedtime.

Suddenly, a whoosh
of wind blew something
tinkly against the
window. Button peeped
around the curtain.

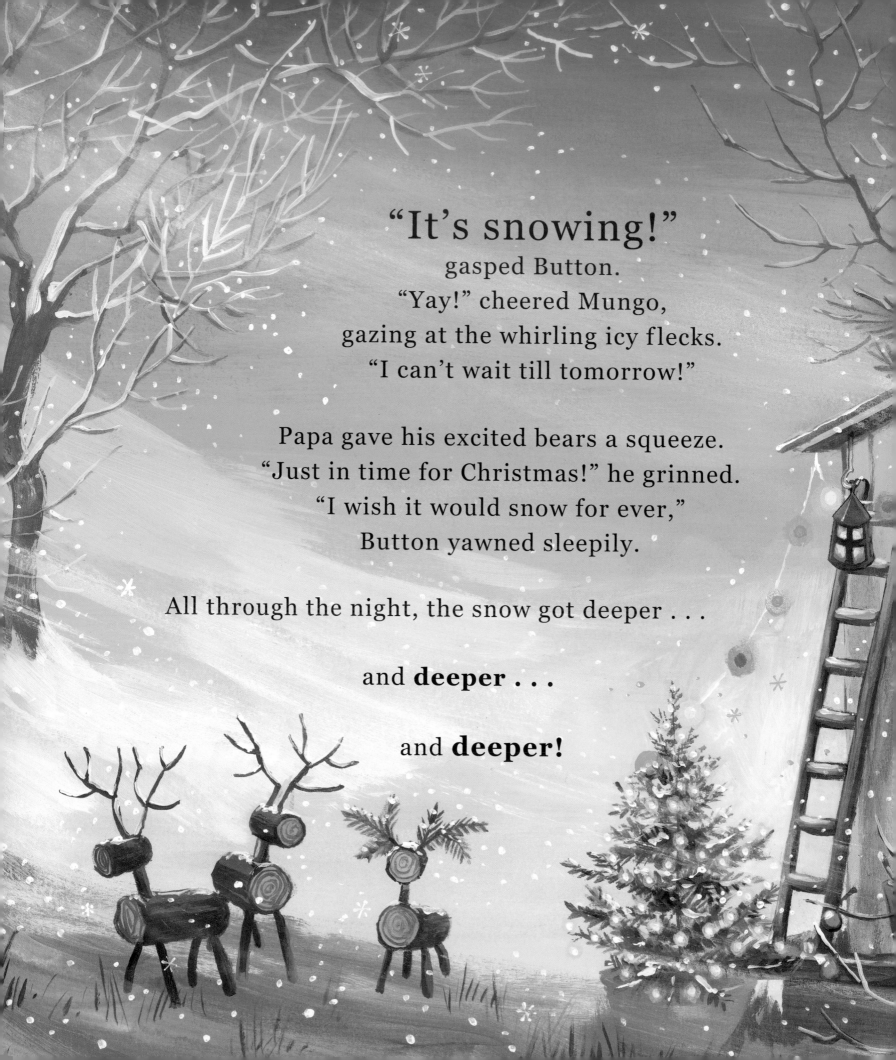

"It's snowing!"
gasped Button.
"Yay!" cheered Mungo,
gazing at the whirling icy flecks.
"I can't wait till tomorrow!"

Papa gave his excited bears a squeeze.
"Just in time for Christmas!" he grinned.
"I wish it would snow for ever,"
Button yawned sleepily.

All through the night, the snow got deeper . . .

and **deeper** . . .

and **deeper!**

The next morning, the family was woken by something falling onto the doormat.

Plop!

"Christmas cards?" wondered Papa.
"I'll get them!" Mungo shouted,
racing off.

But Mungo was in for a big surprise.
"Whoa! Button, look at this!"

A mound of snow had fallen through the
letterbox. "Ooo!" Button whispered.
"Oh my!" exclaimed Papa. "I've never
seen snow do THAT before!"

"Snowball fight!" cheered Mungo, plumping a
pawful into shape and hurling it at Button.
"Oooch!" she squealed, aiming one right back.

But her snowball missed Mungo . . .
and hit Papa!

"Ow!"

"Watch out, bear cubs!" boomed Papa, swinging the biggest snowball of all.

But Mungo ducked, and —

thwump!

— Papa's massive snowball hit the Christmas tree!

"Oops!" he chuckled, leaping to the rescue.
"No more indoor snowballs for us!
Anyone fancy a snack?"

"This will be the best Christmas ever," mumbled Mungo with his mouth full.

"And the snowiest!" giggled Button, finishing her muffin. "Let's go out to play!"

But Button couldn't open the door.

Neither could Mungo.

"We'll climb out the window," decided Mungo. "Come on, Button!" He jumped up to pull the handle, and . . .

Shlump!

An avalanche of white tumbled in!

"Whoohoo! I've got a great idea!" grinned Mungo,
and he began to roll a ball of snow around the floor.
Button joined in, paws patting and eyes widening as the
snowball got bigger and bigger.

"We need a carrot!" called Mungo to the kitchen.
"Still hungry?" replied Papa.

"No, it's for the snowman!" laughed Button.
"Goodness! A snowman indoors!" exclaimed Papa.
"Quick, cubs, let's clear up before he melts into
an enormous puddle!"

The snowflakes drifted down all
morning, and long into the afternoon.
"More snow! More snow!"
sang the bear cubs.

Just then, there was a rumble
from the chimney.
"Is that Santa already?" asked Button.
"It's not night-time yet . . ."
"Quick! Downstairs!" shouted Mungo.
But when they got there . . .

Flooooof!

A humongous pillow of snow plunged down
the chimney and the fire went out.

"Crumbs!" gulped Papa.
"Now this really IS too much snow!"
Even Mungo looked worried.
"If the chimney is blocked,
how will Santa deliver our
presents?" he cried.

"It's all my fault!" sobbed
Button. "I wished it would
snow for ever, and now
THIS has happened!"

"Don't worry," comforted Papa, gathering
up Button in his big bear paws.
"We'll help Santa get through."

"We could use the broom?"
offered Mungo.

"Great idea!" agreed Papa. He squished into the sooty chimney and pushed the broom up as far as he could.

But even on tiptoe, he couldn't reach the top.

"We'll help, won't we, Button?" announced Mungo.

So the bear cubs climbed up onto Papa's shoulders, and with a wriggle and a heave . . .

. . . the broom popped out!
"I can see stars!" squeaked Button.
"Phew!" chuckled Papa. "I think
we've saved Christmas!"

After a good wash,
the three bears cuddled
by the fire.
"Are you sure Santa will
come?" mumbled Button.
"Of course," grinned Papa.

The snow had stopped
falling at last and the forest
looked as glittery as the
pictures in Button's book.

"I love snow,"
she murmured dreamily
as they headed for bed.

And while the bears slept soundly,
Santa climbed down the chimney to leave
them the perfect present.

"A sledge!"
cheered the bear cubs the next morning.
"Just right for the snowiest
Christmas ever!

Wheeeeeeeee!"